To the keeper of this book—it's time for you to visit the magical kingdom waiting within. Believe in yourself—that will give you wings to fly!

Dedicated to Georgia Berry and Freya Berry—
sisters, but also friends forever like Willow and Maya.
May they have many adventures together.
And to their little brother, Teddy.

OXFORD
UNIVERSITY PRESS

Great Clarendon Street, Oxford OX2 6DP
Oxford University Press is a department of the University of Oxford.
It furthers the University's objective of excellence in research, scholarship,
and education by publishing worldwide. Oxford is a registered trade mark of
Oxford University Press in the UK and in certain other countries

Text copyright © Anne Booth 2018
Illustrations copyright © Rosie Butcher 2018
The moral rights of the author have been asserted
Database right Oxford University Press (maker)

First published 2018

British Library Cataloguing in Publication Data

Data available

ISBN: 978-0-19-276623-6

1 3 5 7 9 10 8 6 4 2

Printed in India
Paper used in the production of this book is a natural,
recyclable product made from wood grown in sustainable forests.
The manufacturing process conforms to the environmental
regulations of the country of origin.

Magical Kingdom of Birds

of Birds

The Ice Swans

ANNE BOOTH
Illustrated by Rosie Butcher

OXFORD
UNIVERSITY PRESS

Chapter One

'Maya—don't forget to get ready for skating!' Penny called from the kitchen. 'You'll need a warm coat and hat and gloves, for the outside rink.'

It was Saturday afternoon, when normally Maya and her big sister Lauren would do things together. Lauren had gone away to university now, though, and

Maya's dad and stepmum, Penny, were taking her out for a special treat. The trouble was, Maya didn't want to go.

'I'll never be able to ice skate,' said Maya to her dad in the hallway, knowing Penny couldn't hear. 'I know Penny loved it when she was my age, but she didn't have problems with her legs, like I do. I know I'll just look silly. I'll hate it and I won't be any good, so what's the point?'

'Don't say that, love,' said her dad. 'Look at how good you have got at riding.'

But Maya wasn't listening to him. 'Why did Penny sign me up for those

2

stupid lessons anyway?' she grumbled, pulling on her hat.

'She's worried you are missing your big sister. Penny thought ice skating would be something fun you could do together,' said Dad.

'Are you ready, Maya?' said Penny, coming into the hall. 'Where are your gloves?'

'In my room, I think. I'll go and get them,' said Maya.

'Be quick!' called Penny. 'My friend can't wait to meet you. She is such a great teacher, she'll have you whizzing round the ice rink in no time at all. It's going to be such fun!'

'For you, maybe, not for me,' said Maya under her breath, as she went into her room.

She didn't mean to slam the door quite so hard behind her, but it crashed shut and the satchel on the back of the door fell off. Some pencils and a large book fell out and rolled across the floor.

'Oh no,' said Maya. She managed to pick up the colouring pencils and put them back into the satchel. Then she picked up the book and carried it over to

the table by the window to check it hadn't

been damaged.

'I'm so sorry,' she said to the book. It

was an extraordinarily beautiful book,

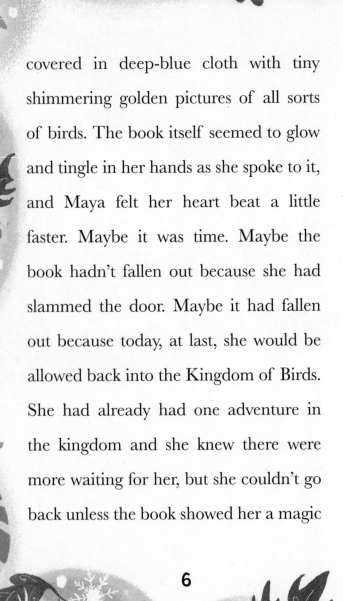

covered in deep-blue cloth with tiny shimmering golden pictures of all sorts of birds. The book itself seemed to glow and tingle in her hands as she spoke to it, and Maya felt her heart beat a little faster. Maybe it was time. Maybe the book hadn't fallen out because she had slammed the door. Maybe it had fallen out because today, at last, she would be allowed back into the Kingdom of Birds. She had already had one adventure in the kingdom and she knew there were more waiting for her, but she couldn't go back unless the book showed her a magic

6

picture to colour in.

'I'd much rather be riding Patch the Magpie than looking silly falling over on the ice,' said Maya, as she picked up her purple woollen gloves and pulled them on. 'I'm the Keeper of the Book, after all, and I need to get back to help Princess Willow regain her kingdom.' She glanced out of the window, and suddenly she saw a big black and white bird fly into the garden. It was a magpie, and it swooped low over the grass and landed just near the window. It tilted its head, its black eyes shining, and seemed to Maya to give her a nod.

My friends must be ready for me, she thought and, taking a deep breath, she opened the book. *Please, magic book, let there be a picture this time.*

Maya had looked in the book every day since she last visited the kingdom, but the pages had been blank. This time, however, she was not disappointed. The book fell open to a picture of an icy tower on a frozen lake. The tower was surrounded by ice sculptures of swans— some big, some very little.

Maya grabbed an ice-blue pencil and began to shade in the tower. She could feel that something incredible was about to happen. Suddenly, all she could see in front of her were whirling, glittering, sparkling, white and black feathers, and a cloud of glittering snow. This was how she had entered the Kingdom of Birds the first time, so she wasn't scared when she was lifted up into the air, and started falling into the picture she had been colouring; tumbling and spinning down into the sparkling magic.

Chapter Two

Maya found herself sitting on the ground, back in the woodland glade where she had first met her friends, Willow and Patch. Her leather satchel was now over her shoulder, with the magical pens safely inside—no doubt this meant she would need them. She put the book back carefully in the satchel. Maya was glad she had already dressed up warmly to go out, as it was cold. Frost covered the grass and the branches of the trees, but somehow the winter scene was not as lovely as it should have been. There was something sad about it.

'Maya! You're back at last!' came a voice, and Maya found herself lifted to her feet and hugged by her delighted fairy friend, Willow. All of the worry she'd felt about ice skating instantly disappeared. It was impossible to stay sad when you were being hugged by a warm-hearted fairy princess.

Willow looked just the same as before, except this time she was wearing a woven hat over her black curls and a cosy-looking cardigan—the cold was even affecting fairies, it seemed.

'Here are your sticks and quiver. We've been keeping them safe,' said Willow, and passed Maya the beautiful wooden sticks that she had made for her, to help her walk in the kingdom. They were so light and useful, and when Maya was riding Patch she had used their hooked tops to get them out of a few tricky situations.

'Welcome back, Maya!' said Patch, the handsome magpie, who, in the Kingdom of Birds, was bigger than Maya and the perfect size to ride on. He bent his head so she could stroke his smooth, glossy feathers. His special saddle and harness were already on, so Maya knew they would soon be soaring up in the sky together, on a new, exciting adventure. Lord Astor, Princess Willow's evil uncle, had stolen the kingdom from her and destroyed the magic feather cloak which gave her power. Patch and Willow had told Maya that there was an ancient prophecy, that a girl would come from the human world to save the Kingdom of Birds from danger. She would be the keeper of an enchanted book, and ride on the back of a magpie. Princess Willow and Patch were so relieved Maya was that girl, and had asked her to help them restore the magic feather cloak.

This is better than silly ice skating, any day, thought Maya, happily.

'We're so glad you are here,' said Willow. 'And it's good that you are wearing warm clothes, as I am afraid it is only going to get colder.'

'We have heard rumours that Lord Astor has built a secret, magical ice tower and plans to somehow turn the whole kingdom to ice unless he is accepted as king,' said Patch. 'The problem is, nobody seems to know exactly where it is.'

'I coloured in a picture of a tower to get here,' said Maya. 'Look!' As she spoke, she noticed that her breath was making clouds in the air.

'We have no time to waste,' said Willow. 'It is getting colder every minute.'

Maya found a tree stump to sit on, took out the book from her satchel, and opened it. Patch and Willow looked over her shoulder at the picture of the ice tower.

'That looks like Swan Lake to me,' said Patch. 'But why didn't any of the swans fly across and warn us?'

'Why are there all those statues of swans in the picture?' said Willow. 'I don't remember them before.'

'Has Lord Astor put them up as a thank you to the swans for working with him?' asked Maya.

Willow frowned, and her beautiful brown eyes looked serious. 'I can't believe that. Swans have always been particularly loyal to the crown. There has always been a beautiful marble fountain on the shores of Swan Lake, to symbolize our friendship. It has a statue of a fairy and a swan carved on it. I've never seen any other statues. And these ones look as if they are on the surface of the water. It's all very odd.'

'Well, there's only one way to find out what is going on,' said Patch. 'Get on my back and let's fly, Maya!'

Maya grabbed hold of the saddle and

pulled herself up onto Patch's back. She couldn't wait to fly with him again. When she moved through the air with Patch, Maya felt confident and balanced in a way she didn't feel on her own two feet.

Patch prepared for take-off. He bent his head, stretched out his wings, ran forward a few steps . . . and then they were up, soaring into the sky behind Willow! Maya loved the funny feeling in her tummy as they rose quickly into the air—it was such an exciting feeling, like when she had gone on a rollercoaster at the fair.

Maya was glad Penny had reminded her to get her gloves. Penny had knitted them and her hat, and they were so soft and warm. It was still very cold though. She leant forward, so she could get some warmth from Patch's body, and looked down on the kingdom from between his beating wings.

It looked so beautiful as they flew across the snow-covered landscape, above frosted trees and icy streams, pretty and sparkling in the winter sunlight. Bright, chattering flocks of parakeets flew in the distance—it was strange to see them

away from green trees and hot summer days. The red-breasted robins who flew up to say hello and pay their respects to the princess were a more familiar sight. The robins didn't seem to notice anything being wrong, but Maya knew the book would not have shown her Swan Lake if they were not supposed to go there.

Maya and Patch and Willow flew through a pass between white-topped mountains, their shadows long on the snowy ground far below them. Maya found it thrilling to listen to eagles calling in the air and look up to see their wide-winged silhouettes wheeling high above them. She heard the beating of their huge wings as they swooped down and flew around the group. It was breathtaking to be so close to such majestic birds; to see their intelligent eyes and sharp talons and enormous wingspans, as they flew beside them. Maya was glad the eagles came in peace, as their friends, as it was hard not to be overawed by their sheer strength and power.

'Welcome, Princess Willow, and Patch, magpie brother,' they called. 'Welcome back, Maya, Keeper of the Book—long heard of and waited for. May good fortune go with you.'

Maya felt proud that such magnificent, stately birds knew who she was, but she was glad that she wasn't there by herself. She was quite intimidated by how grand they were.

'I thank you, esteemed eagles,' answered Willow, regally. 'Do you know anything about what is happening with the swans?'

'I regret I cannot tell you,' said the largest eagle, seriously, 'but we know that since Lord Astor took your throne, things

have been going wrong. Recently, there is a cold in the air that we have never felt before. Even we—who know the snowy mountains so well—feel a new chill, deep in our bones, that can only mean bad news.'

'Why won't he live in harmony with the birds, the way fairies are meant to?' said Willow. 'He even has a bird name— Astor means "sparrowhawk". It's a noble name, but he doesn't live up to it.'

'From our high vantage point, we can see that all is not well across the kingdom, and as we ride the air currents we can feel that the cold is coming from the direction of Swan Lake. We wish we could come with you to help, but some force seems to keep us by this mountain, and we feel a weariness creep in as we fly.'

'The swans must really be in trouble,' said Willow, looking worried. 'We must go. I bid you good day, and hope to see you again.'

'Fly well!' called the majestic birds. Maya looked up and watched as they soared away against a wintry, clear-blue sky.

'The eagles are such magnificent flyers,' said Patch, admiringly, 'but even they seem to be flying more slowly than usual.'

'I know what they mean about feeling the chill in their bones,' replied Maya. 'I can feel it myself.'

'The sooner we get there the better,' said Willow.

Chapter Three

As they flew on, snow began to fall and the landscape below became whiter and whiter. They passed over a pine forest, and saw a flock of tiny birds flying frantically around between the Christmassy-looking trees.

'Fly lower!' called Willow, 'I want to see what is the matter.'

They swooped
down into the forest
itself, and Maya saw that
there were lots of tiny birds flying in and
out of the trees. The birds were grey-
green in colour, with black and yellow
stripes on their heads. It should have been
a pretty sight, but the little birds seemed
worried.

'What is the matter, goldcrests?' asked
Willow.

'It's so cold, Princess Willow—we are
looking for food,' tweeted the birds.

'We have to build up our

30

strength; we are trying to
eat enough food during the
day so we can survive the even colder
night. The poor wrens have given up
already.'

In the bare trees, some little
wrens were too cold to look
for any more food. Instead
they were huddling together
for warmth. They were so tiny that Maya
counted more than ten in one little group.
Willow flew up and put her arms around
the feathery bundle to give
them a reassuring hug.

'I'm very sorry you are so cold and miserable. The Keeper of the Book is here, so don't lose heart, little birds. She is here to help us, and we are going to defeat Astor,' said Willow. The little birds were too cold to talk—they just moved even closer together, in their little freezing feathery group.

Willow shivered a little as she flew back to join Maya and Patch in the air.

'Are you all right, Willow?' said Maya.

'Fairies don't usually feel the cold too much, as our wings and our flying keep us warm. But this cold is different. It gets inside you and makes you feel sad as well as cold. This freezing winter Astor is spreading over the kingdom has no warmth or fun. Like him.'

They heard a screeching call and saw a colourful brown, blue, black, and white bird flash past.

'Greetings to you, cousin jay,' called

Patch. The jay doubled back.

'Patch—am I glad to see you!' said the jay. 'Lord Astor wants us to follow him, and says he won't lift the cold spell until we agree. We have held out against him so far, but we can't carry on much longer like this,' he continued. 'In the autumn, I buried the acorns I gathered, but now the snow is too deep for me to find them. The smaller birds have to eat every day, and they are losing energy fast. I tell you—'

'I'm sorry to interrupt you, cousin,' said Patch, 'but I think we'd better fly on.

It is urgent that we challenge Lord Astor as soon as possible, and the snow is getting heavier.'

'Of course, cousin,' said the jay. 'I don't know if you have noticed the wrens, but—'

'We have, thank you,' said Willow. 'Thank you so much.'

Maya thought it was a bit mean of Willow to cut off the jay like that, but the situation really did feel urgent. The snow was falling thickly all around them, and it seemed like they were still a long way from Swan Lake.

'He's a good chap, but he is so terribly chatty,' said Patch. 'It's funny, because he is so shy with strangers and hides in the woods normally, but once he starts talking it's hard to stop him!'

The group flew on, over more rivers and valleys and hills. They flew across flat, snow-blanketed treeless moors, where the white snow below them lay smooth, undisturbed, and untouched, like Christmas-cake icing. Maya thought she spotted some birds way down on the ground, but, before she could be sure, a blizzard blew in around them.

The snow fell so fast and thick that soon Maya could not see anything. She had to keep blinking, as the cold wet snowflakes blew in her eyes, and she held tightly on to Patch. Willow had completely disappeared from view.

'Willow! Are you there?' called Maya, into the cloud of whirling snowflakes. It was frightening to be surrounded by such whiteness and not be able to make anything out.

'Yes,' called Willow, her voice muffled as she called through the snowstorm. 'But it is so hard to fly.'

'Princess—climb on my back with Maya,' panted Patch.

'Where are you?' called Willow. 'I can't see anything.'

'Grab hold of my stick,' shouted Maya, holding it out in the direction she thought Willow's voice was coming from. 'Use it to find us.'

She felt the stick jolt as Willow grabbed the end and made her way along it to Patch and Maya. Maya grabbed the freezing little fairy princess and pulled her on to Patch's back, but the big, brave magpie was tiring in the storm. The three friends felt themselves blown back and forth, and Patch tipped sideways as Maya and Willow grabbed on to each other and tried to stay on.

'I can't go on much longer,' shouted Patch, his wings beating more and more slowly as they lost height and started descending. 'I don't know where we are or what we will land on.'

'Help!' shouted Willow. 'If there are any birds out there in the storm, I, Princess Willow, ask for your help!'

Suddenly they heard, far away, a mewing whistle, as well as a noise which reminded Maya of geese honking and dogs barking. Then there was a series of low, deep hoots, getting nearer and nearer, more and more of them, all around. Two large, ghostly white bird shapes emerged out of the blizzarding snow and flew directly under Patch, lifting him up. There were loud clacking sounds.

'Snowy owls!' said Willow, in relief. 'Thank you!'

Held up by the steady owls, Patch kept on course through the blizzard, and they emerged from the worst of it. As the snow turned into flurries and then finally died away altogether, the birds left Patch to fly by himself and flew up beside them, where Maya could see them clearly. They were lovely to look at—one was pure white and the other had a speckling of darker feathers. Both had yellow eyes and dark bills, which they snapped open and shut, making the clacking sound Maya had heard in the storm.

'Welcome, Princess Willow,' the speckled one said. She was the female snowy owl. 'You are very much needed. Bad things are happening in your kingdom.' She snapped her bill shut again.

'Even we, who are so used to snow, want this to stop,' said the male—the larger, pure-white owl flying beside them, his wings bright. 'Lord Astor is up to no good, and we hear from other birds that the evil seems to be centred around Swan Lake, which is near here. We have tried to fly there to see what is happening, but we keep getting caught up in blizzards like this one,' he hissed angrily. 'We would go with you now, to help you, but first we need to rest. Lately we have been so tired, exhausted in a way we never normally are.'

'We cannot wait for you, brave birds— we have to get to Swan Lake as soon as we can,' said Willow. 'But we can never thank you enough for saving us.'

'Thank you,' said Patch. 'I am feeling much stronger now, thanks to your help. I don't know what we would have done without you.'

'Farewell,' hooted the owls, as they flew down to perch on a tree stump.

The group flew on through freezing, snowless air. Patch's feathers got colder and colder as they flew, and Maya gave a little shudder. When would they arrive? How would they ever get warm?

'Look!' cried Willow, pointing, and suddenly they saw the blue ice tower on a frozen lake, surrounded by statues of swans, just like the picture in the book. From high in the air, they could see how the ice was spreading slowly and steadily from the edges of the lake, so that everything it touched was covered in white.

'We've got to stop this!' said Maya.

Patch swooped low and, folding his

wings, came in to land next to a tall, elegant fairy with white hair and a white dress, who was sitting by the lakeside, crying.

'Whatever is the matter, Snowdrop?' said Willow.

'Oh, Princess Willow, I am so glad to see you!' said Snowdrop, wiping her eyes and putting her glasses back on. 'Lord Astor has turned all the swans to ice, because they tried to stop him freezing the lake.'

Maya gave a horrified gasp. 'So those are not ice statues, they are real birds,' she said. 'Poor things! It looks like he has even frozen the swan babies too—look at all those poor little cygnets in a line.'

'I must help my subjects,' said Willow, darting towards the nearest frozen swan.

'No! Come back, princess! You mustn't touch them, or you will be turned into ice too!' called Snowdrop, flying after Willow and grabbing her by the hand.

But it was too late. There was a flash of ice-blue light, and Snowdrop and Willow were frozen in flight. Willow had touched an enchanted swan, and Snowdrop had touched her—so now,

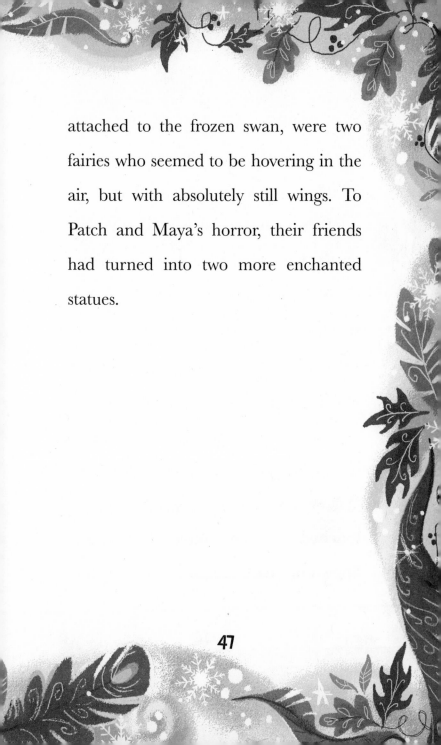

attached to the frozen swan, were two fairies who seemed to be hovering in the air, but with absolutely still wings. To Patch and Maya's horror, their friends had turned into two more enchanted statues.

Chapter Four

'Oh no!' said Maya. 'Patch, what are we going to do?'

Patch took off and they flew around Willow and Snowdrop, careful not to even let a wing tip touch them. It was no good. They were beautiful, sparkling ice statues, and it was impossible to know if they could even see or hear what was going on. Maya and Patch would have to defeat the evil Lord Astor alone.

Patch flew back to the lakeside. Suddenly they heard the loud, mocking laughter of Lord Astor as he flew towards them, accompanied by fairy guards.

'I like my niece better as an ice statue,' he said. 'And I'm glad you've seen me defeat her, once and for all. I've enchanted the ice so the cold will spread, and before the end of the day this kingdom will be under my power. There is nothing a silly magpie and a human girl can do to stop me.'

Maya noticed Lord Astor was wearing a fur cloak and a strange new crown on his head. The crown was white and spiky, like icicles, with a huge, white sparkling diamond in the centre.

Lord Astor saw her looking and smiled an unpleasant smile.

'It might be fun to leave you free for a little bit longer, so you can see me take over the kingdom. But you'd better get out of here before I change my mind.' He touched the white diamond in the centre of the crown, and Maya saw blue sparks fly out of it and into his fingers.

'Go on—get out!' snarled Lord Astor, and he fired a cold, blue ice-blast at them from his hand. Patch saw it coming and flew up quickly so that it missed.

'Watch this ice show while you can,' Lord Astor called after them. 'You'll be part of it yourselves soon—you and anyone else in the Kingdom of Birds who doesn't accept that I am the rightful ruler!' Then he flew away to the ice tower.

Patch flew towards a tree by the lakeside, and perched on a branch. Maya slid off his back and sat beside him. He spread out his wing protectively and they cuddled up close, cold and sad, like the little wrens they had seen in the forest.

'We need to ask the book what to do,' said Maya. 'It helped us before, so surely it can help us this time too.' Maya was shivering a little as she spoke, and it wasn't just with the cold. Willow made every adventure seem fun, and that made it seem possible to do impossible things, but without her it was different. It was hard to be brave and positive, when you had seen your best fairy-friend turned into ice.

Maya took the book out of her satchel, and it opened again at the picture of the ice tower. Maya delved into the bag for a pencil, and a deep-blue one jumped into her hand and then seemed to guide her hand to an outline of a small door she hadn't noticed before, at the very top of the tower.

'The book knows something, anyway,' said Patch. 'That's a good sign. It looks like you have to colour the door in.'

As soon as Maya had coloured the door blue it began to open, and magical light came sparkling through it. As Patch and Maya watched, the page turned, and there was the door close up, filling the new page. It revealed Lord Astor standing in the frame, wearing the icicle crown. He had a sneer on his proud face, but Maya noticed that he hugged himself as if he was cold, even though his fur cloak looked heavy and warm and reached the ground.

The blue pencil dropped into the satchel and a white pencil rolled into Maya's fingers.

'But the page is white already,' said Maya, as her hand was pulled to the diamond in the middle of Lord Astor's spiky icicle crown. She started colouring it in anyway, and as she did, it began to sparkle and glow, each facet of its many sides winking and shining with a pure light. It was beautiful, and just colouring it in made Maya feel happier and braver.

'It's something to do with the diamond

in the crown,' said Maya. 'Do you know what it is, Patch?'

'I think I do,' he replied. 'I remember, when I was a baby magpie, my mother used to tell me stories about sparkling things, before I went to sleep at night. She told me a story about the sparkliest diamond of all—the diamond of the Swan Lake fountain. The swans have good, pure hearts, like the diamond, and every winter the swans use the diamond's power to freeze the lake for the winter ball, so that everyone in the kingdom can have fun. Normally, the cold never leaves the water, and the surface of the lake is covered with stalls and even bonfires. Birds and fairies dance and have fun, and everything looks sparkly and wonderful. I remember the day I was old enough to go to see it for myself. It was such a happy event. Lord Astor must have stolen the diamond from the fountain, and created the icicle crown to harness its power. Only someone with a cold heart like his could use the good, pure diamond in such a horrible way.'

'We've got to get the diamond back, Patch, and destroy the crown.' said Maya.

'The blue door must be a clue. We have to open it.'

They looked at each other. It was so much scarier without Willow in charge, and knowing that she and Snowdrop had been frozen made it seem all the more dangerous. Maya looked again at the sparkling diamond on the page. It gave her hope.

'Come on, Patch,' she said. 'We can do this. We've got to save Willow and the others. We must break the enchantment of Swan Lake.'

Maya could feel the beating of Patch's heart and her own, as they prepared to fly. It was not easy to get back up on him from the branch, but Maya knew she didn't need to have strong legs—she remembered what she had learnt from riding ponies. She leant on him and grabbed the saddle as she pulled herself up by her hands, and soon she was safely on his back.

'Well done, Maya. Let's go!' he cried, spreading his wings, and they took off, swooping over the frozen lake towards the castle. Already they could see cold tentacles of frost rising up from the surface of the lake, from the enchanted water and the statues. Patch dodged the scary fronds weaving up towards them, and they finally reached the blue door and the balcony. Patch hovered in the air.

'What next?' he said.

'I suppose I'd better try the handle,' said Maya, leaning towards the door. 'Maybe we can fly inside the castle.' But before she could get to it, the door flew open and Lord Astor walked out on to the balcony. The diamond was white and glowing brightly.

'Quick, Maya! Grab the crown!' cried Patch, and she leant towards it with her hands outstretched.

Lord Astor noticed what she was trying to do and yelled furiously, 'Get out of here!' He put his hands up to the diamond, pointed his fingers at Maya and Patch, and started aiming magical ice-blasts at them.

Maya lay flat against Patch's neck as he flew away, swooping and diving. He avoided the crackling blue ice-waves, but kept circling the tower.

'Shall we go back to shore, Maya?'

63

Patch said.

'No, there's no time to waste. We have to stop him,' she replied, pulling out a stick from her quiver. 'Can you swoop down fast, and fly low over his head? I have a plan.'

'I can try!' said Patch. 'Here goes . . .'

Chapter Five

Maya had never known Patch to fly so fast. First, he put all his energy into soaring high above the castle—so high that Lord Astor must have thought they had flown away.

'Ready, Maya?' he said, hovering in the air. 'Hold on tight. I'm going down!'

Then, like the fastest fairground ride

ever, they hurtled down towards the balcony, where Lord Astor stood, staring up at the sky. Maya gripped her stick firmly, holding it so the hook was at the far end.

'Please work,' she said to herself.

Suddenly they reached the balcony. Patch slowed for a split second, right in front of Lord Astor, whose eyes widened in shock as Maya hooked the top-heavy crown from his head.

'Guards! Guards!' screamed Lord

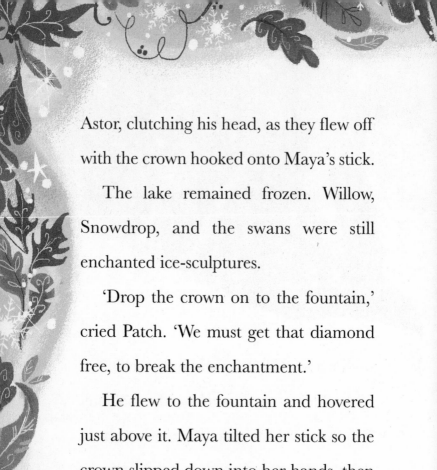

Astor, clutching his head, as they flew off with the crown hooked onto Maya's stick.

The lake remained frozen. Willow, Snowdrop, and the swans were still enchanted ice-sculptures.

'Drop the crown on to the fountain,' cried Patch. 'We must get that diamond free, to break the enchantment.'

He flew to the fountain and hovered just above it. Maya tilted her stick so the crown slipped down into her hands, then she took it and threw it as hard as she could at the statue of the fairy and the swan. It hit against it and smashed into smithereens, the diamond rolling out and onto the ice.

At that moment, there was a huge cracking sound and the ice lake began to melt.

'Quick, get the diamond, before it sinks into the lake and is lost for ever!' said Patch. He flew low to the ground. Maya held on to his reins and bent down to pick up the glowing jewel from among the ice shards and put it in her satchel.

The ice tower collapsed and fairy guards flew out of every window. Lord Astor flew around in the air, waving his arms and shouting at them.

There was the sound of beating wings as, one by one, the black swans and the white swans imprisoned in the ice were freed from its magic. They ran across the lake towards Lord Astor, in an angry, honking, trumpeting flock.

Lord Astor turned and shook his fist in rage at Maya and Patch. They heard him shout something like, 'I'll get you for this,' and, 'interfering girl . . . meddling magpie!', but he didn't have time to say much—he was too busy flying as fast as his fairy wings could take him away from the furious swans.

Maya looked over to Willow and Snowdrop, frightened that they might still be trapped under the enchantment. In front of her eyes, they transformed, flying up in the air and straight over to her and Patch, who were waiting by the fountain.

'Thank you so, so much,' said Willow, throwing her arms around her friends.

Once Lord Astor was a small speck in the distance, the swans turned around and flew back towards them too. Two particularly elegant swans, one black and one white, came forward from the rest of the crowd and bowed their long, elegant necks.

'Princess Willow, thank you for coming to save us,' said the black one, a beautiful female.

'We are for ever in your debt,' said the white swan, an elegant male.

'I did nothing,' said Willow. 'It was my dear friends, Maya, the Keeper of the Book, and my faithful magpie, Patch, who saved you.'

'I want to see them! Me! Me! Me!' peeped some fluffy cygnets, pushing

themselves out from between the legs of the adult swans.

'Children, your manners! I am so sorry—the children are a little excited,' said their mother. 'But we are all so grateful to you for freeing our diamond.'

'Indeed—thank you, Maya, Keeper of the Book, and Patch the magpie,' said the white male. Both swans bowed their necks before them.

'Where is the diamond now?' said Snowdrop, in alarm.

'I have it in my satchel,' said Maya, bringing it out. There was a huge sigh of relief from the waiting swans. Maya went to pass it to Willow, but Willow shook her head and smiled, pointing at the marble fountain. There, plain to see, was a place for the diamond, right between the carved marble swan and the carved fairy.

'You go and put the diamond in its place in the fountain, Maya,' said Willow. 'You are the one who rescued it.'

Maya dismounted from Patch's back and, using her sticks to help her walk, approached the two large swans, who had flown to either side of the fountain. Close up, they were awe-inspiring, and Maya felt shy in front of such stunning birds.

'Replace the diamond, human child,' they said together, and Maya stepped forward.

Chapter Six

Maya carefully slotted the diamond in its rightful place in the fountain, and there was a loud chiming sound. Some of the swans made loud bugle calls of delight. The little cygnets made funny, high trumpet sounds, trying to copy the adults.

'Legend says that this pure and elegant ice-diamond was entrusted to the keeping of swans long, long ago, because of our own pure hearts, and our loyalty to each other and to the fairy kingdom,' said the black swan, solemnly. 'As long as its power is used to encourage and delight, there is no cause to fear it.'

'It is when its great power is used for the wrong reason, by the wrong people, that it is to be feared,' said the white swan. 'Lord Astor would have been destroyed by it, had he kept it and kept using it wrongly. His cold heart would have become colder, until he would have turned to ice himself.'

The sound of low hoots could be heard in the distance, and the two snowy owls flew towards them, their wings powerful but noiseless in the air.

'Princess Willow,' they called joyfully as they landed. 'The spell is broken! We hear, carried on the air, the news that the deep evil cold has ended all over the kingdom. Now there is only beauty in the snow and we can fly easily again, free from the deep, freezing poison in our bones!'

'Thank you, snowy owls,' said Willow. 'You will be given great honour in our history, for rescuing us from that terrible blizzard.'

'We swans will always be in your debt, dear owls,' said the black swan. The white owls bowed respectfully to both of them and to the princess.

'Thank you—you saved our lives,' said Maya. The owls looked at her with their striking, cat-like, yellow eyes. Maya thought they were amazing birds to look at.

'It is our honour, Keeper of the Book,' they said solemnly.

'Can we have a party now?' interrupted the cygnets, and everyone laughed.

'Swans—approach!' commanded the large white swan, and a group of black swans, and white swans, and white swans with black necks, approached the throne and touched their beaks to the diamond. As each beak touched the white diamond, it sparkled like the jewel itself.

The sun was beginning to set, and in the twilight the graceful forms of the swans flying over the lake was an impressive sight. Some of them were gliding over the water, swimming around each other in a beautiful dance. They bent their necks to touch the surface of the lake with their glittering beaks, and lines of silver ice flowed down from them, creating intricate snowflake patterns.

'It's so lovely,' sighed Maya.

'Fly with us, Keeper of the Book!' said the white swan. 'Come, climb on my back.'

When Maya was settled, with a thrumming of his wings, he ran in powerful strides across the lake and soared up in the air, his wife flying beside them.

Maya looked down, as more and more patterns appeared. They soon disappeared as the lake covered over with ice again. This time it was not the sinister, blue ice of Lord Astor's doing, but silvery-white and sparkling. Maya looked over at Willow and Patch and the snowy owls flying with them, and beamed with delight at how pretty it all was.

Other swans flew above the lake and circled each other in a ballet in the air, touching beaks so that magical sparks, like fireworks, formed and joined together to form magic lanterns, suspended in the air. Night had fallen now and, in the dark, the whole lake glowed with the silver ice and sparkled in the light of the lanterns.

'Come on to the ice!' called the little cygnets. They rushed onto it themselves, slipping and falling over and laughing and having lots of fun.

'We swans fly easily in the air, and swim easily on water, but it is good for us all to do something different from time to time,' laughed the black swan. She glided down onto the ice with the cygnets. The white swan flew back to the shore, Maya still on his back.

Maya dismounted and, leaning a little on her sticks to give her balance, turned to face the huge swan.

'Thank you,' she said, shyly. She had met lots of regal birds on her journey to Swan Lake, but she didn't think she would ever get used to being so close to them.

'No, thank *you*, Keeper of the Book, we are for ever in your debt,' said the white swan, solemnly. 'Now, I invite you to celebrate with my family and take to the ice.'

'Come on, Daddy!' called the cygnets excitedly.

The swan laughed. 'Duty calls!' he said, and stepped onto the ice, skating carefully but gracefully over to his waiting family.

'I can't do this,' said Maya, in a panicked whisper to Willow. 'I don't even have skates.'

'No problem!' laughed Willow, and she flew over to a willow tree. The fairy princess spoke softly to it and it extended its branches. Maya watched as Willow used the leaves and twigs to magically weave ice skates for Maya and her and Snowdrop. Even Patch, who did not have webbed feet, got his own willow skates.

'We love it when the swans throw an ice party,' laughed Willow, putting on her skates. 'You'll see—birds and fairies will spread the word and come from far and wide to join us.'

'Come on, Maya!' cried the laughing

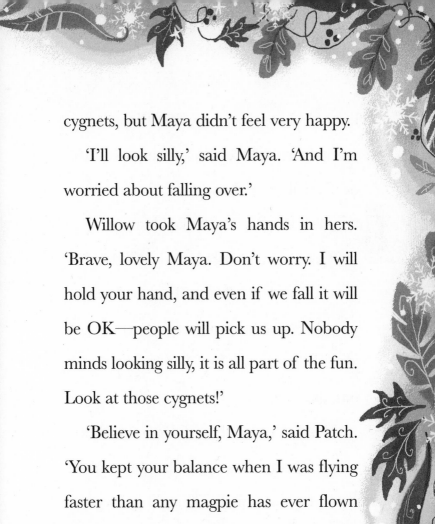

cygnets, but Maya didn't feel very happy.

'I'll look silly,' said Maya. 'And I'm worried about falling over.'

Willow took Maya's hands in hers. 'Brave, lovely Maya. Don't worry. I will hold your hand, and even if we fall it will be OK—people will pick us up. Nobody minds looking silly, it is all part of the fun. Look at those cygnets!'

'Believe in yourself, Maya,' said Patch. 'You kept your balance when I was flying faster than any magpie has ever flown before,' he added, unable to resist a boast. Willow finished attaching his skates and he took a step onto the ice, slipped, and immediately fell over. Willow and Snowdrop nearly fell over themselves, they were so busy laughing as they picked him up.

'Come on, Maya,' said Willow, her brown eyes kind. 'We will go as slowly as you like—and you can stop whenever you like—but give it a try. You might find it fun, after all.'

Hand in hand, they glided onto the ice, which by now was full of laughing fairies and excited birds. Giggling cygnets skated and fell over, and more sedate, older swans glided along the ice, looking elegant and serene.

'We all fell over when we were learning,' called the mother swan encouragingly, as she skated past, her beautiful black feathers glossy against the white ice.

Patch had found his feet and was showing off a bit, doing figure of eights in the centre, in front of admiring cygnets. Maya just felt relieved to go around the circle of the lake. Willow held one hand, and Snowdrop held the other. At first, Maya wasn't used to her legs moving so fast—she stumbled a little, but Willow and Snowdrop caught her each time.

She began to relax and enjoy herself. They did fall over a few times, but the main reason was not because her legs gave way but because she and Willow and Snowdrop were laughing so much.

When Maya got tired, she and Willow joined Snowdrop and the other fairies at the lakeside, where she sat by the warm fire. Fairies and swans and owls were toasting marshmallows on sticks and handing them round. Fairies were passing around mugs of hot chocolate from a magic hot-chocolate fountain, and everyone was smiling and laughing. This wasn't the cruel, cold, scary ice-world Lord Astor had wanted, this was a happy world of fun and laughter, where nobody minded falling over and everybody helped each other up.

Willow and Maya were sitting together by the lakeside, cuddling some very tired cygnets. They were listening to Patch telling them the bedtime story his mother used to tell him about the wonderful diamond of Swan Lake, when the large black and white swans approached them.

They left two feathers, one white and one black, at Maya's feet.

'We know that Princess Willow needs swan feathers for her cloak, so we present these to her now, on behalf of all swans,' they said together.

Maya looked at Willow and Patch.

'I suppose that means it is time to go?' she said, sadly.

'Yes, you need to put the feathers in the magic book, and take them back to your human world to keep them safe,' said Willow, giving her a hug. 'Thank you so much, yet again, dear Maya, for all you have done for The Kingdom of Birds. Do not worry—you will return. We need you to help us collect more feathers. There are many more adventures in store. What fun we will have!'

'Thank you, Maya,' said Snowdrop.

'Thank you, Maya,' said the swans.

'Goodbye, Maya,' said Patch. 'See you soon, I hope!'

'Goodbye, Patch,' said Maya, hugging him.

The fluffy cygnet brothers and sisters were now sleeping in a happy heap, cosy and warm by the fire after their exciting day. Maya pulled out the book from her satchel, took a deep breath, and carefully placed the black and white feathers on a blank page.

Instantly, the page began to glow, and the lake and the swans and the fairies and Patch all disappeared. Maya found herself falling through the air again, first through clouds of glittering, silver snow and sparkling black and white feathers, but then through feathers that were all the colours of the rainbow, and she found herself back in her bedroom.

Chapter Seven

There was a knock on her bedroom door.

'Maya,' came Penny's voice. 'May I come in?'

'Hang on a minute!' replied Maya.

The book was in front of her, and the open page showed a beautiful, colourful scene of the ice party at Swan Lake. Bright ice-lanterns hung magically in the air, and the swans and fairies were skating on the lake. Even the cygnets were there! Maya was so happy that she had joined in, it had been such fun. As she smiled, the two feathers on the page turned into drawings, and Maya closed the book.

'Come in!' called Maya, and Penny poked her head around the door. Her usually cheerful face was looking worried.

'Maya, I'm so sorry if I've forced you to go for this skating lesson, against your will. My friend has lots of practice teaching people, and she is sure she can help you to do it. But I can see it's worrying you, and that's not what I want at all. I thought it might be fun, but I can cancel it now, if you like.'

'No, Penny,' said Maya. 'I'm sorry I was so grumpy. I knew you were being kind, but I was scared about falling over and feeling silly. I'm so much more confident sitting down and riding.' She smiled, as she thought of Patch and their amazing flight above the lake.

'I know—I realize that now. I'll go and ring my friend right away, and cancel,' said Penny.

'No, don't,' said Maya. 'I'm not feeling

scared of it any more. It's just a new thing to learn, and I can't get better at it until I try. I'd like to have a go. I can always stop if I don't like it, but I'll never know until I try.'

'Really?' said Penny. 'Honestly? I don't want you to feel you have to, just because I organized it.'

'No, I'd like to try with you, now. I think it will be fun. Honestly. It'll be fun,' said Maya, and she found she really believed it.

'Oh Maya!' said Penny, a big smile on her face. 'I'm so glad. I felt awful at the idea that I was forcing you into something you weren't happy about. You must promise me to always tell me if you don't want to do something.'

They gave each other a big hug.

'I know how much you miss Lauren now she is at university, and I hoped doing new things would help you feel better,' said Penny.

'You're right, Penny,' said Maya, looking over at the book on the table. She was thinking of all the wonderful new things she had already done and would do in the Kingdom of Birds, and the friends who were waiting for her there.

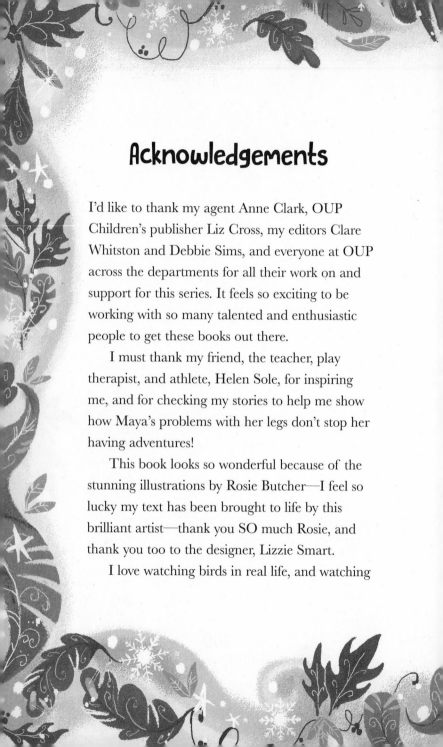

Acknowledgements

I'd like to thank my agent Anne Clark, OUP Children's publisher Liz Cross, my editors Clare Whitston and Debbie Sims, and everyone at OUP across the departments for all their work on and support for this series. It feels so exciting to be working with so many talented and enthusiastic people to get these books out there.

I must thank my friend, the teacher, play therapist, and athlete, Helen Sole, for inspiring me, and for checking my stories to help me show how Maya's problems with her legs don't stop her having adventures!

This book looks so wonderful because of the stunning illustrations by Rosie Butcher—I feel so lucky my text has been brought to life by this brilliant artist—thank you SO much Rosie, and thank you too to the designer, Lizzie Smart.

I love watching birds in real life, and watching

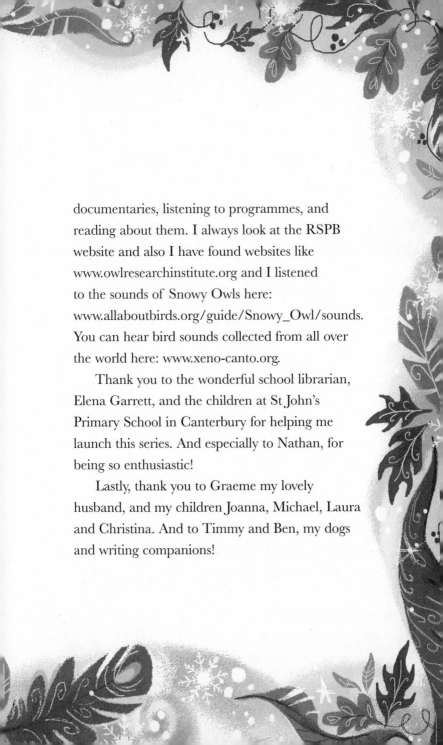

documentaries, listening to programmes, and reading about them. I always look at the RSPB website and also I have found websites like www.owlresearchinstitute.org and I listened to the sounds of Snowy Owls here: www.allaboutbirds.org/guide/Snowy_Owl/sounds. You can hear bird sounds collected from all over the world here: www.xeno-canto.org.

Thank you to the wonderful school librarian, Elena Garrett, and the children at St John's Primary School in Canterbury for helping me launch this series. And especially to Nathan, for being so enthusiastic!

Lastly, thank you to Graeme my lovely husband, and my children Joanna, Michael, Laura and Christina. And to Timmy and Ben, my dogs and writing companions!

About Anne

Every Christmas, Anne used to ask for a dog. She had to wait many years, but now she has two dogs, called Timmy and Ben. Timmy is a big, gentle golden retriever who loves people and food and is scared of cats. Ben is a small brown and white cavalier King Charles spaniel who is a bit like a cat because he curls up in the warmest places and bosses Timmy about. He snuffles and snorts quite a lot, and you can tell what he is feeling by the way he walks. He has a particularly pleased patter when he has stolen something he shouldn't have, which gives him away immediately. Anne lives in a village in Kent and is not afraid of spiders.

About Rosie

Rosie lives in a little town in East Yorkshire with her husband and daughter. She draws and paints by night, but by day she builds dens on the sofa, watches films about princesses, and attends tea parties. Rosie enjoys walking and having long conversations with her little girl, Penelope. They usually discuss important things like spider webs, birds, and prickly leaves.

Bird Fact File

Turn the page for information
on the real-life birds that
inspired this story.

Fun Facts

Find out all about these
beautiful majestic birds

1. Swans usually mate for life.

2. An adult male swan is a cob, and
a female is a pen.

3. The English word 'swan' is derived
from Indo-European root 'swen',
meaning to sing.

4. Swans are among the largest flying birds.

5. Swans' wing spans can be over 3.1 metres.

6. Swans can reach a length of over 1.5 m and weigh over 15 kg.

7. The Northern Hemisphere species of swan have pure white plumage but the Southern Hemisphere species are mixed black and white.

8. Although birds do not have teeth, swans have beaks with serrated edges that look like small jagged 'teeth'.

9. Swans are almost entirely herbivorous, though they may eat molluscs, small fish, frogs, and worms.

10. A group of swans is called a bevy or a game when on the ground, and a wedge when in flight.

11. In the water, food is obtained by up-ending or dabbling.

12. Unlike many other ducks and geese, the male helps with the nest construction.

13. Swan eggs take between 35 and 42 days to hatch.

14. Swans can fly as fast as 60 miles per hour (nearly 100 km/h).

15. The swan has over 25,000 feathers on its body.

16. Swans' quills were used for feathering arrows.

17. In England, the Queen owns all mute swans.

Where do you find
swans?

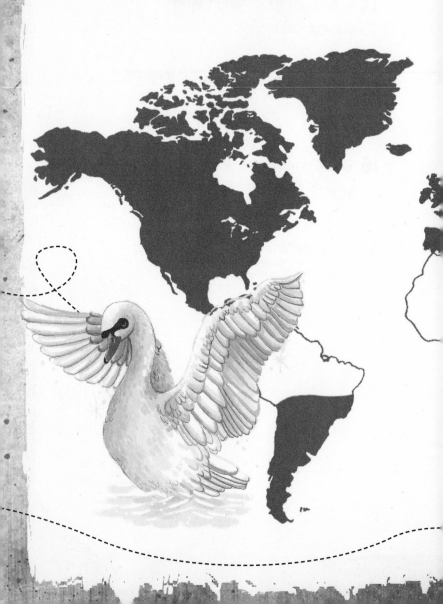

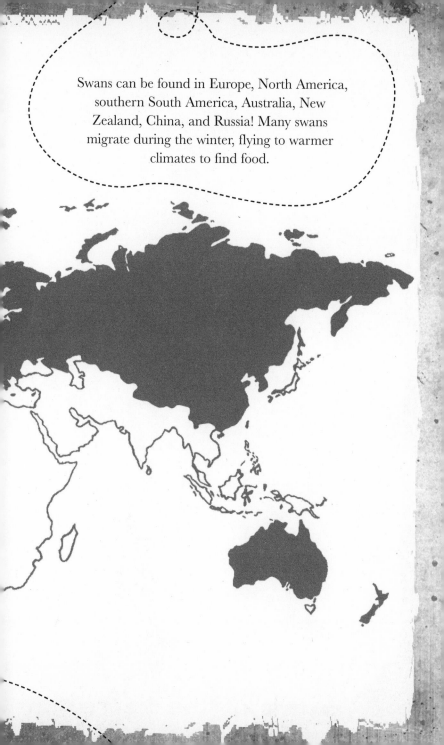

Turn the page for some fantastic

Bird activities

Make an origami swan

Why not try making your own swans,
out of paper?

Origami paper works best as it's a bit
thinner, so it's easier to fold. Plus you can
get lots of pretty colours!

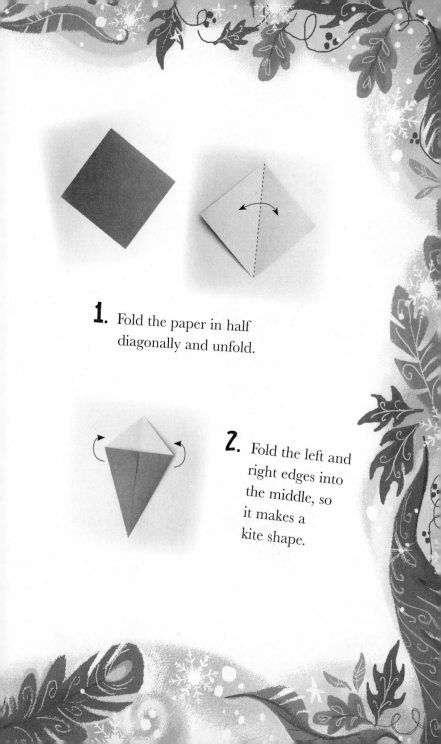

1. Fold the paper in half diagonally and unfold.

2. Fold the left and right edges into the middle, so it makes a kite shape.

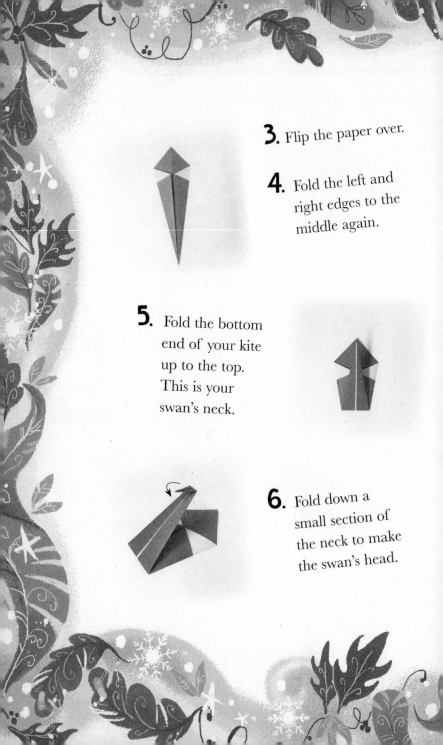

3. Flip the paper over.

4. Fold the left and right edges to the middle again.

5. Fold the bottom end of your kite up to the top. This is your swan's neck.

6. Fold down a small section of the neck to make the swan's head.

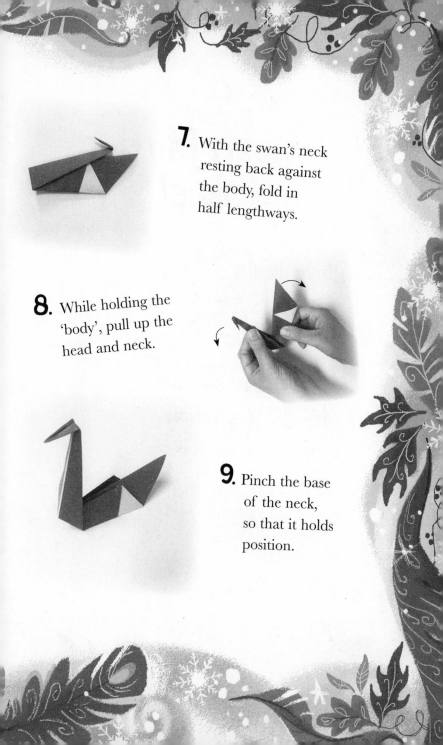

7. With the swan's neck resting back against the body, fold in half lengthways.

8. While holding the 'body', pull up the head and neck.

9. Pinch the base of the neck, so that it holds position.

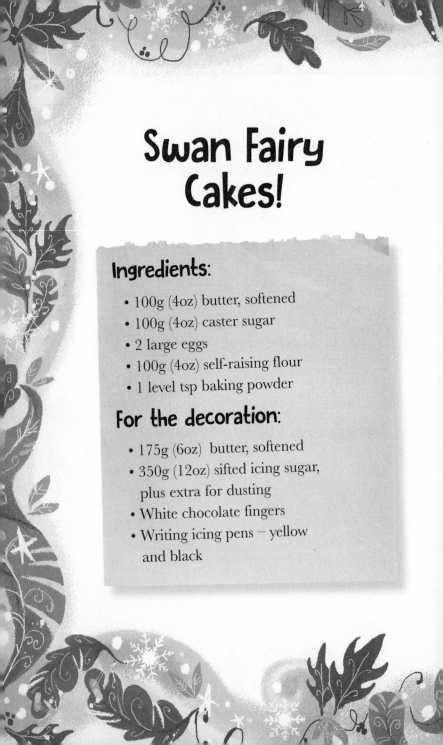

Swan Fairy Cakes!

Ingredients:

- 100g (4oz) butter, softened
- 100g (4oz) caster sugar
- 2 large eggs
- 100g (4oz) self-raising flour
- 1 level tsp baking powder

For the decoration:

- 175g (6oz) butter, softened
- 350g (12oz) sifted icing sugar, plus extra for dusting
- White chocolate fingers
- Writing icing pens – yellow and black

You will need:

- Weighing scales
- Bowl
- Sieve
- Whisk
- Fairy cake cases
- A 12-hole bun tin
- Piping bag

Step 1

Preheat the oven to 200°C/Fan 180°C/gas 6.

Step 2

Place fairy cake cases into a 12-hole bun tin.

Step 3

Measure all the cake ingredients into a large bowl and beat well for 2–3 minutes until the mixture is well blended and smooth.

Step 4

Fill each paper case with the mixture.

Step 5

Bake for 15–20 minutes or until the cakes are well risen and golden brown. Lift the paper cases out of the bun tin and cool the cakes on a wire rack.

Step 6

To make the icing, beat the butter and icing sugar together until well blended.

Step 7

Cut a slice from the top of each cake and cut this slice in half.

Step 8

Pipe a swirl of butter cream into the centre of each cake and place the half slices of cake on top to resemble swan wings.

Step 9

Place half a white chocolate finger into the buttercream to form the swan's neck.

Step 10

Draw on eyes and a beak with the writing icing pens.

Join Maya for another adventure in
The Sleepy Hummingbirds

Evil Lord Astor has a plan to capture and cage the tiniest residents of the Magical Kingdom of Birds, the hummingbirds. Will Maya be brave enough to save the day?

Magical kingdom of Birds

The Sleepy Hummingbirds

ANNE BOOTH

Illustrated by Rosie Butcher

Chapter One

Maya was sitting in her bedroom, watching a magpie hopping around the garden.

'I heard that when you see a magpie on its own it isn't unlucky for you, it is just unlucky for the magpie because they don't have a friend. So I hope you are lucky and find a friend soon,' Maya said out loud, looking through the glass and out at the handsome black and white bird. Even though he was in the garden, he tilted his head as if he had heard her, and gave a little hop.

'I'm feeling lonely too, Magpie,' said Maya. 'My big sister Lauren is going away to university, and today is her last day at home. I am going to miss her SO much.'

Somehow it helped, saying it out loud. The bird came nearer, looking up at her as if he could understand what she was saying.

'Dad and Penny and Lauren are rushing around, packing up the car and charging up and down the stairs with bags and lamps and things,' Maya went on. 'I'm just getting in the way, and I don't want Lauren to see me feeling sad. She is so excited.'

Maya went over to the pot of peanuts she kept for the garden birds, and then opened the window to get the bird feeder she had stuck on the glass, and topped it up. Instead of being scared by the window opening, the magpie hopped even closer.

'You're beautiful,' said Maya.

Maya loved birds. Her room was full of pictures of them. She had a bird mobile over her bed, binoculars for bird spotting, and lots of books and DVDs about them. Her pencil case had birds on it, her pyjamas and nighties had birds on them, and even the clock on her bedroom wall played a different bird call every hour during the day. Luckily it switched off at night!

One good thing about having a ground-floor room was that Maya could see the garden birds really well. As well as the bird feeder on the window, there was a bird table right outside. She had already put out fat balls for the birds, because the migrating birds needed to build up energy before their long flight south. Maya knew which birds migrated and which visited or stayed over winter; she knew what special food each type of bird ate, and she spent lots of her pocket money on treats for them.

There was a knock at the door.

'Maya, can I come in?' came Lauren's voice.

'Yes,' said Maya, trying to sound more

cheerful than she felt. She knew that Lauren was so happy to be going away to university, and she wanted to be glad for her, but she couldn't help feeling that nothing was going to be the same any more. Lauren was the best big sister ever.

'Hey, Maya, are you OK?' said Lauren, coming in holding something behind her back.

Maya smiled and nodded, but a big tear escaped and rolled down her cheek.

'Oh Maya—don't cry!' said Lauren. She quickly hid something behind the curtain and went over to Maya to give her a big hug. 'I'll be back before you know it. And I've even got a ground-floor room, like you, so it will be easy for you to visit. It looks onto the university lake, so we'll be able to watch the birds together. I think there might be ducks!'

Maya laughed. Lauren was always showing her funny videos of ducks, and Maya had drawn a duck on Lauren's good luck card. Maya loved drawing birds.

'Now, close your eyes and put out your hands,' said Lauren.

Maya put out her hands and felt

something heavy and flat being put on them. She opened her eyes and saw it was just a simple, brown leather satchel.

'Open it,' said Lauren, smiling.

Maya looked inside the bag and took out what was there. She gasped. It was the most beautiful book she had ever seen. The cover was made from a deep-blue cloth with tiny gold birds all over it, and in gold lettering the title said *The Magical Kingdom of Birds*. There were pictures of birds all over the cover, back and front: birds in trees, in forests, in gardens; birds flying over the sea, soaring over mountaintops, diving into rivers; in deserts, in snow; birds in palaces and birds in cottages. Each picture was wonderful in its detail, and the birds were of all different shapes and sizes. Maya had the strangest feeling when she looked at each tiny scene, that it was getting bigger as she gazed at it. It was almost as if she was zooming in on it, like when she looked through her binoculars. She blinked and the pictures went back to normal, but Maya had a funny feeling inside, a feeling that something amazing was going to happen.

She opened the book. The first page had a detailed picture in black and white, of a very proud-looking magpie standing in a woodland clearing.

'It's a colouring book!' said Lauren. 'There are some special colouring pencils to go with it in the bag too. Look, there is something written inside the front cover.'

Maya looked away from the picture of the magpie to the writing.

To the Keeper of this book—it's time for you to visit the magical Kingdom waiting within. Believe in yourself—that will give you wings to fly!

'It's amazing!' said Maya. 'Where did you get it?'

'From Mum,' said Lauren. 'She gave it to me.'

'Oh Lauren—you can't give it to me, if Mum gave it to you,' said Maya, feeling sad. She wished she could remember her mum the way Lauren could. She had only been little when their mum had died.

'No—you don't understand,' said Lauren. 'Mum gave it to me, with the bag and the pencils, when she was ill and you were a toddler. She said to put it aside safely until you were older, so I put it at the back of my wardrobe. I was just sorting out things for university and felt like now was the right time to give it to you. I hadn't even opened it until today. It's beautiful, isn't it? It's amazing that Mum gave you a bird book when you were a baby, and you know so much about birds!'

'I know!' said Maya. She didn't expect to suddenly feel so happy and excited. Penny was the best stepmother anyone could have, but it was special to know that her mum had been thinking of her, and had got her this book when she was just a baby. How had her mum known she would grow up loving birds so much?

This sad day was turning to something new and wonderful, and Maya knew, deep down, that it was somehow because of this special book.

There was a tap on the window. The magpie was now perched on the back of the garden seat, so that he was really close to the glass.

'Cheeky thing!' laughed Lauren. 'Look, I'll be back later. Sorry we're rushing around so much. I thought you might like to start colouring in a picture while you're waiting. Dad's taking us all out to dinner once the car is packed.'

Lauren left Maya with the book and the bag and the pencils, and Maya hugged the book to her chest.

'Thanks, Mum,' she whispered.

She went to her table by the window. The magpie was still looking in at her.

'Look, there's a big picture of you on the very first page,' she said, holding it up to the window for the magpie to see. 'I wonder what other birds are in it.' She turned the pages. Oddly they were all blank, and, odder still, the book itself kept flicking back to the first page, as if it didn't want her to go any further.

'This is a strange colouring book,' said Maya.

The magpie tapped the glass again. He gazed at her with his shiny black eyes and put his head on one side. Maya had the funniest feeling that both the book and the magpie were telling her to 'get on with it'.

'Well, I won't have to worry about colouring you in wrong!' She laughed. 'You can be my model if you stay still.'

The magpie hopped up and down on the spot, but didn't fly off. He seemed to be watching her.

Maya reached into the bag for the black pen, and started to colour in the book magpie's feathers . . . but as soon as the first feather was finished, something amazing happened. Suddenly, all Maya could see were twirling, tiny, sparkling feathers—first black and white like the magpie's, but then all sorts of browns and reds and oranges and yellows and greens and blues. The glowing feathers swirled around her and somehow she fell into the picture she had been colouring, tumbling and spinning until she found herself sitting, holding the book, on soft green moss in a woodland glade. Next to her was the magpie, now much taller than her. Looking at the flowers and plants around her, Maya could see that it wasn't the magpie who had got bigger, but she who had got smaller.

'It worked! It really worked!' cried a voice, and Maya turned to see a little fairy emerge from underneath a bush. 'The Keeper of the Book has come at last!'

Ready for more great stories?

ANNE BOOTH

Making a wish for a Christmas miracle.

Lucy's Search for Little Star

THE NEW ADVENTURES OF MR TOAD

Operation Toad!

TOM MOORHOUSE

with pictures by HOLLY SWAIN

HORACE & Harriet

Take on the Town

WRITTEN AND ILLUSTRATED BY THE SPLENDIFEROUS CLARE ELSOM

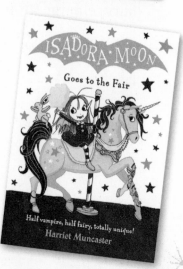

ISADORA MOON

Goes to the Fair

Half vampire, half fairy, totally unique!

Harriet Muncaster